Bedrock Press™
A T L A N T A
Published by Bedrock Press
An imprint of Turner Publishing, Inc.
A Subsidiary of Turner Broadcasting System, Inc.
1050 Techwood Drive, N. W.
Atlanta, Georgia 30318

Printed in the U. S. A.
First Edition 10 9 8 7 6 5 4 3 2 1
ISBN   1-878685-66-X
Library of Congress Catalog
Card Number 93-61335

Distributed by Andrews and McMeel
A Universal Press Syndicate Company
4900 Main Street, Kansas City,
Missouri 64112

DK DIRECT LIMITED
Managing Art Editor Eljay Crompton
Senior Editor Rosemary Mc Cormick
Consultant Dr. Mark Collins
Writer Rachel Wright
Illustrators Hanna-Barbera, Inc.,
Myke Taylor, Kate Canning, Jane Cradock-Watson
Designers Diane Klein, Marianne Markham

YOGI'S
BIG JUNGLE
ADVENTURE

Bedrock Press™
A T L A N T A

"DEAR READER"

This book has been created especially for you. It's guaranteed to provide fun, adventure, and fabulous nuggets of information. And the fascinating facts – just like the residents of the jungles – come in all different shapes and sizes. Join Yogi Bear and Boo Boo on a guided tour of the mysterious jungles of the world. There are pictures bursting with beautifully colored animals, birds, and flowering plants. We hope you enjoy this exciting adventure, and we look forward to having you join us on another Fantastic Discovery.

CONTENTS

INTO THE JUNGLE

Yogi Bear and Boo Boo invite you to join them on an amazing jungle adventure. Follow them as they walk toward a jungle where the trees are so tall they seem to hold up the sky, and the leafy treetops stretch far into the horizon. Feel the warm, sticky air on your face and watch the rain clouds as they gather high above the trees.

Now step closer, into the shade of the trees – step into the jungle.

Jungle Spots
The shaded green areas on the map show where most of the world's tropical jungles are found.

Full of Life
More animals, insects, and birds live in jungles than anywhere else on Earth. A four-square-mile area of jungle can contain 400 kinds of birds, 60 sorts of frogs, and 42,000 different types of insects!

Giant Trees

Most jungle trees grow to be between 80 and 120 feet tall. But the tallest trees are called emergent trees. They can grow to be over 150 feet high!

Can't See the Forest for the Trees

Jungles contain hundreds of different kinds of trees because most plants grow best in sunny, rainy places. Two and a half acres of jungle may have as many as 200 kinds of trees.

Rain and Shine

Tropical jungles are only found in areas close to the equator. In these steamy parts of the world, there are no hot and cold seasons. The weather is warm and wet all year.

Jungles are full of overlapping layers of trees. Nearly all jungle trees are evergreens, shedding their leaves and growing new ones all the time.

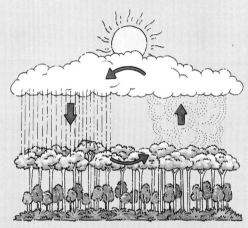

Rain water is heated by the sun. As the water warms, it changes into vapor and rises into the air. There, the droplets in the vapor join together and form rain clouds.

Tropical jungles provide us with a rich variety of foods such as bananas, mangos, coconuts, avocados, and nuts.

EQUATOR: An imaginary line around the middle of the Earth that divides the Northern and Southern Hemispheres.

THE JUNGLE FLOOR

The jungle floor is almost completely dark because the sun is hidden by the tangled branches above. The air is hot and still, and the ground is covered with dead leaves. Although leaves fall from the trees all year, they never build up into huge piles because they either rot away or insects eat them. Looks like Yogi's found a tasty snack – do you know what it is?

Gone Hunting
Like many forest-floor animals, bush dogs are not good at climbing trees. Instead they hunt small animals on the ground.

Root Food
As leaves rot they are broken down into minerals that are then taken up by the trees' roots.

Ant Farmers
These leaf-cutter ants are carrying bits of healthy leaves back to their underground nest.

Spreading Out
Many big jungle trees have mighty roots spreading out from their trunks. These roots help to keep the trees steady by spreading the weight of each tree over a wide area.

Creeping and Crawling
A million kinds of insects have been discovered in the world's jungles. There are many more still to be found!

Leaf-cutter ants are the farmers of the insect world. They chew the leaves they bring back to their nests into a mush. Then they grow a fungus on the mush, which they eat.

Jewel Beetle

Lacy Stinkhorn Fungus

Cup Fungus

FUNGUS: Any living thing that is like a plant but has no leaves, flowers, or green coloring, and can't make its own food as plants can.

LIVING IN THE MIDDLE

Jungle plants and animals need each other to survive. Animals feed on plants and then spread their pollen and seeds for them.

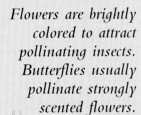

Flowers are brightly colored to attract pollinating insects. Butterflies usually pollinate strongly scented flowers.

Violet-cheeked Hummingbird

The middle layer of the jungle is called the understory. It is a shady place, where there is just enough light for small trees. Some of these trees are fully grown, while others are young trees that need more sunlight before they can get any taller. They often have to wait until one of the bigger trees comes crashing down and lets more light through before they can reach full size.

Here I Am!
Some flowers sprout from tree trunks so that birds, bats, and insects can find them more easily.

Drip, Drop!
Many jungle plants have waxy leaves that point downward so that rainwater can flow off them.

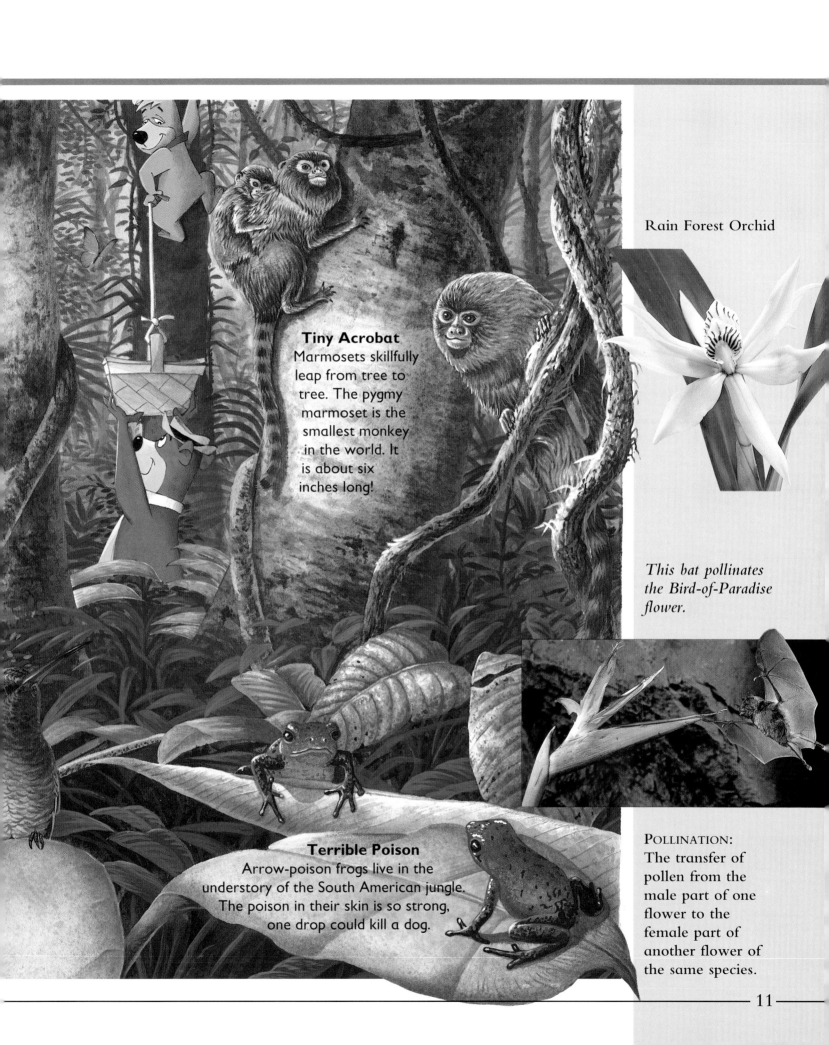

Rain Forest Orchid

Tiny Acrobat
Marmosets skillfully leap from tree to tree. The pygmy marmoset is the smallest monkey in the world. It is about six inches long!

This bat pollinates the Bird-of-Paradise flower.

Terrible Poison
Arrow-poison frogs live in the understory of the South American jungle. The poison in their skin is so strong, one drop could kill a dog.

POLLINATION: The transfer of pollen from the male part of one flower to the female part of another flower of the same species.

LIFE AT THE TOP

U p here, in the topmost layer of the jungle – the canopy – it is bright and breezy and always noisy! Parrots squawk at each other, and swinging monkeys howl to defend their homes. Many jungle creatures live in the canopy because there are lots of things to eat. Because they live so high up, they have become skillful acrobats. Looks like they've taught Yogi and Boo Boo how to hold on tight!

Parrots know who's who because they recognize the special colors and patterns of each other's feathers.

Toucans live high up in the canopy. They use their big, hollow beaks to pick fruits and berries.

Balancing Act
South American monkeys, such as the howler monkey, can use their tails like an extra arm or leg.

THINK TWICE
Color helps animals to find each other or to hide from predators. How many animals can you think of who use color to attract each other or to protect themselves from their enemies?

Up, Up, and Away!
Many of the emergent trees produce wing-like seeds. On windy days, the seeds flutter away from the parent tree. Where they land, new trees may grow.

Colorful Friends
Many jungle birds have flashy-colored feathers. Bright feathers help birds "talk" to each other.

Slothful
Sloths cling onto branches with hook-like claws. When they move, they go very slowly.

Giant Blue
There are more butterflies in the South American jungle than anywhere else on Earth. With its wings open, the giant blue morpho measures seven inches across.

Large Birdwing Swallowtail

Blue Morpho

Some animals are in danger because their jungle homes are being destroyed.

Homerus Swallowtail

This beautiful Quetzal is eating a piece of fruit.

SLOTH: A shaggy-coated, slow-moving animal of South and Central America that lives in trees.

THE FLOODED FOREST

Jungle jaguars are good swimmers and have been known to catch and eat crocodiles!

The giant anaconda weighs as much as a fully grown gorilla.

When the water rises in the Amazon River, dolphins swim among the tree roots.

Not all piranhas are meat-eaters. Some, like this pacu, are vegetarians.

VULTURE: A large bird of prey related to eagles and hawks that eats dead animals.

I'm the King
The king vulture is the only vulture to live in the jungle. It has a keen sense of smell, which it uses to find food.

Snake Alert!
The giant anaconda is so strong it can squeeze a caiman to death! The anaconda is the heaviest snake in the world.

Greedy Guys
The Amazon contains about 3,000 different kinds of fish. Some of them eat plants and seeds. Others, such as the red piranha, prefer fish or land animals. Hundreds of hungry red piranhas can eat a large animal in minutes!

The biggest jungle in the world is the Amazon Jungle in South America. It is nearly the same size as Australia, and it flourishes mainly along the lowland that surrounds the great Amazon River. Each year the Amazon, and the smaller rivers that run into the Amazon, burst their banks. Parts of the jungle become covered with water, and fish swim among the trees. Yogi and Boo Boo think this may give a whole new meaning to the term "Gone Fishing!"

Gone Fishing
This jaguar is on the lookout for a fish dinner. As soon as a nosy fish swims near its tail, the jaguar will scoop it up.

Step on Me
These giant water lily leaves grow on long stalks that rise up from the river bed.

Surprise, Surprise!
This caiman – a close relative of the alligator – floats like a log just below the water's surface, waiting for a thirsty animal to stop for a drink. Then, SNAP! It grabs the animal with its mighty jaws, and drowns it before eating it.

SWINGING THROUGH THE ASIAN JUNGLE

The Asian jungle stretches across southeast Asia, south China, part of India, Indonesia, and down to the northern tip of Australia. It covers mountains, lowlands, and islands. One of the most useful plants to come from this jungle is the rattan. Its rope-like stems are used to make all sorts of things, from furniture to hats. They're strong enough for Tarzan, and little Boo Boo, to swing from!

Leaf-eating Giants
A fully grown Indian elephant weighs as much as five cars — about 11,000 pounds. They spend most of their time eating leaves, which they grab with their trunks.

Tiger Manners
Tigers prefer to sneak up on their prey. They also like to drink with their meals, so they drag their prey to the water's edge before eating.

Flower Power
The Rafflesia flowers of Indonesia are the biggest flowers in the world. Each one measures about three feet across. That's four times wider than this page!

Swinging Along
Like other apes, orangutans have no tails. They use their great dangling arms to swing through the trees, and their long, bendy toes to hold onto the branches.

Brain Power
Apes, such as orangutans, are some of the most intelligent animals in the world. The name orangutan means "man of the forest."

Most emergent trees are about the same size as a 20-story building. But there are five kinds of jungle trees that grow even higher. All of them are found in Asia. The tallest one is the tualang, which may grow to be 272 feet high.

Believe it or not, there are flying frogs in the jungle. But they don't actually fly – they glide. To make sure they land on the right branch, they steer in the air with their webbed hands and feet.

PREY: An animal hunted and killed by another animal for food.

EXPLORING THE AFRICAN JUNGLE

In Africa, people living in or near the jungle eat a variety of wild animals. Part of their diet includes porcupines, caterpillars, termites, grasshoppers, and the giant African snail!

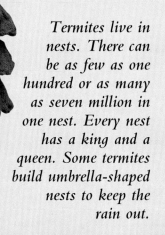

Termites live in nests. There can be as few as one hundred or as many as seven million in one nest. Every nest has a king and a queen. Some termites build umbrella-shaped nests to keep the rain out.

A queen termite can lay up to 30,000 eggs a day!

CHIMPANZEE: An African ape smaller than a gorilla, with hands adapted for knuckle-walking.

The African jungle has many exciting animals, including the gentle gorilla and the super-smart chimpanzee. Gorillas and chimps live in groups, give birth to one baby at a time, and "talk" to each other using different sounds. Like Yogi and Boo Boo, they eat a wide variety of foods such as fruits, nuts, and berries. Although they are wild, and sometimes aggressive animals, they can be very friendly and playful with each other.

Looking Good
Chimps and gorillas "groom" their babies' fur with their fingers to keep it bug-free and tidy.

Hunting Prey
This leopard is waiting for lunch to pass by so that it can drop down on the animal's back and kill it.

Nice Guy
People used to think that gorillas were fierce and frightening, but this is not true. They only get mean if one of their family is in danger, or if they are hurt.

Clever Chimps
Chimps use different tools to help them hunt for food. This chimp is using a stick to scoop termites out of their nest.

Mighty Beetle
One of the largest insects in the world lives in the African jungle. The African goliath beetle is more than five inches long.

THE JUNGLE AT NIGHT

Yogi and Boo Boo have discovered that the jungle is not the place to go if you want a peaceful night's rest! While some animals go to sleep when it's dark, others are just waking up. Animals that are awake at night are called nocturnal animals. They often have large eyes or a good sense of smell to help them look for food in the dim light. (Some also have big ears so that they can hear the faintest sound.)

"Eye" Spy
A tarsier's eyes, like those of many other nighttime creatures, are big and saucer-shaped, to let in as much light as possible.

Making Sense
Insect-eating bats use their keen hearing to find prey at night. Fruit bats use their good eyesight and sense of smell.

Night Life
Some understory flowers only open at night. Their sweet-scented smell attracts nighttime moths.

Geckos are small, nocturnal, tropical lizards. Just like people, their pupils open up wide in the dark to collect light. But like other nocturnal animals, geckos have a special layer in their eyes which can collect even more light.

Colugo Travel
The colugo glides through the air like a paper plane.

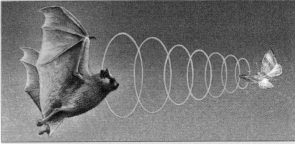

As they fly through the night, insect-eating bats make squeaking sounds. If the sound waves of these squeaks hit an insect, they bounce back toward the bat's ears as an echo. The length of time this echo takes to return tells the bat how far away the insect is.

The Snout Family
The tapir has a supersensitive snout. It uses it to find leaves and roots to eat. It also uses its snout like a finger to pull food near to its mouth.

COLUGO: A flying lemur. It has a broad fold of skin on both sides of its body to help it to glide.

TAPIR: A large pig-like animal with hoofs and a flexible snout. All tapirs are endangered.

LIVING IN THE JUNGLE

Imagine that you have been asked to live in a jungle. You are surrounded by snakes and creepy-crawlies, and there is not a store in sight. Could you survive? To us, jungles seem wild places, but, as Yogi and Boo Boo have found out, people have lived in them for thousands of years. Some gather seeds and hunt animals. Others plant crops. Like all jungle people, the Pygmies of Africa know their forest well.

Looking the Other Way
If neighbors disagree, they sometimes move the doorways of their huts, so they no longer face each other.

Scary Stories
Some Pygmies love to tell tales of evil forest spirits, to keep strangers out of their part of the jungle!

Hunting Tips
Small groups of Pygmy hunters use poison-tipped arrows to shoot monkeys and rodents. Larger groups use nets and spears to catch big animals.

Pygmies collect honey from 17 kinds of bees. They collect the honey in different ways. Sometimes they use smoke to drive the bees away. Sometimes climbers scale trees using a belt for balance.

Pygmy gathering wild honeycombs.

Elephants are a big help to Pygmies. They dig up earth in search of salt, encouraging plants to grow. Wildlife eat the plants, and Pygmies eat the wildlife!

Trading Post
Pygmies often trade with other Africans. In return for meat and honey taken from the forest, the Pygmies are given cooking pots, knives, and cereal.

PYGMY: One of a group of jungle-dwelling peoples living in Africa who are all less than five feet tall as adults.

RODENT: Any of a small group of animals with large front teeth that are used for gnawing. Rats and mice are typical rodents.

THE DISAPPEARING JUNGLE

The burning jungles are visible from space.

J ungle alert! The world's jungles are disappearing – and disappearing fast. People have been cutting down huge numbers of trees for wood. They have also been burning the jungles to make way for roads, buildings, and farms. If they don't stop chopping and burning soon, rich forest soils will be at risk, local climates will change, and many of the animals, plants, and people that you have met in this book will disappear forever.

Every minute, a piece of jungle the size of a football stadium is destroyed.

After logging, the land is often cleared for farming.

CARBON DIOXIDE: A heavy, colorless, odorless gas present in the atmosphere or formed when fuel containing carbon is burned.

Wise Words
The Pygmies of Africa have a saying: "When the jungle dies, so shall we." Let's hope that this never happens.

Sea of Change
When trees are burned, they release a gas called carbon dioxide. As this gas builds up, it traps heat from the sun. If too much heat gets trapped in our atmosphere, the weather will get warmer. Icecaps may start to melt and sea levels may rise.

People Power
There are people in the world who want to save the jungles. They have set up parks where no one can cut down trees.

THINK TWICE
Can you think of ways we might be able to help save the world's trees? Perhaps you could begin a paper recycling program in your school!

The Rosy Periwinkle is used in cancer research.

Flooding Problem
When jungles are destroyed, the soil is left unprotected. Over time, rain washes the soil away into rivers, which become clogged with mud. During rainstorms, the blocked-up rivers overflow and villages are flooded.

The Moreton Bay Chestnut is used in AIDS research.

Quinine is used to cure malaria.

The jungles of the world contain special plants that may cure certain illnesses. It's important that these plants do not disappear.

25

BRAINSTORM

WHERE DO I BELONG?
As you have discovered, animals live in different parts, or layers, of the jungle. Look at the jigsaw pieces below and match, or fit, each animal piece to the piece in the layer where it would live.

Art Time
Design a
Save the World's
Wildlife poster.

NATURE TRAIL
The next time you explore your backyard or your local park try to identify the trees, plants and flowers you see. Is there wildlife you can observe? Keep a notebook and record your findings.

THINK TANK
Why do some animals have colors that blend with their environment? Why are some animals brightly colored?

QUESTION TIME

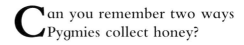

Can you remember two ways Pygmies collect honey?

The destructon of jungles causes flooding. How does this happen?

Why are flowers brightly colored or strongly scented?

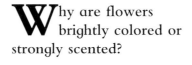

Where would you find the biggest jungle in the world?

What kinds of animals would you find in the African jungle?

What are the names of the three main layers of the jungle?

What is the name given to nighttime animals?